HarperCollins®, ✿®, HarperFestival®, and Festival Readers™
are trademarks of HarperCollins Publishers Inc.

Maurice Sendak's Little Bear: Little Bear and the Missing Pie
© 2002 Nelvana
Based on the animated television series *Little Bear* produced by Nelvana.
™Wild Things Productions
Little Bear Characters © 2002 Maurice Sendak
Based on the series of books written by Else Holmelund Minarik and illustrated by Maurice Sendak
Licensed by Nelvana Marketing Inc.
Printed in the U.S.A.
Library of Congress catalog card number: 2001092494
www.harperchildrens.com

2 3 4 5 6 7 8 9 10

First Edition

Little Bear and the Missing Pie

BY ELSE HOLMELUND MINARIK

ILLUSTRATED BY CHRIS HAHNER

HarperFestival®
A Division of HarperCollins*Publishers*

On a crisp fall day, Little Bear
and his friends made piles of leaves
and then scattered them all around.

"Let's play hide-and-seek,"
said Little Bear.
"I'm *it!*"

Just then, Mother Bear set a pie

on the windowsill to cool.

"Ooh," said Hen, "it smells so good!"

"And it looks so yummy!" said Duck.

"I could eat it all up!" said Emily.

7

"This is a special pie for Father Bear,"

said Mother Bear.

"It's his favorite."

"We have a game to play!"
said Little Bear, impatiently.
"Start hiding! One, two, three,
four, five . . ."

"Hen! I see you!" said Little Bear.

"I was just smelling that pie," said Hen.

"I'll hide now."

"Six, seven, eight, nine, ten!"
cried Little Bear.

"Ready or not, here I come!"

Little Bear spun around.

The pie was gone!

"Owl, the pie is missing!"

cried Little Bear.

"*Hoot!*" cried Owl.

"We must look for clues and find it."

"I see a feather,"
said Little Bear.
"Maybe that is a clue."

Little Bear pulled on the feather.

"Quack!" cried Duck.

"Oh, I'm sorry, Duck,"

said Little Bear.

"I thought you were a clue!"

"Duck, what is on your face?"

asked Owl.

"Where were you hiding?"

asked Little Bear.

"I was in the raspberry bushes!"

said Duck.

Someone must have been very hungry,
for most of the berries were gone.

Little Bear licked Duck's face.

"It's raspberry!" he said.

"Of course!" said Duck.

"When you are near raspberries—
you eat them!"

"Look!" said Duck.

"What's under that bush?"

Little Bear and Owl followed Duck.

"It's Emily's shoe!" said Duck.

"But where is Emily?"

asked Little Bear.

From up in the tree came a voice.

"Look up here, Little Bear!

My shoe fell off when I was

climbing this tree."

It was Emily.

There she sat, high up in the tree.

Emily climbed down.

Little Bear looked at

Owl, Duck, and Emily.

Who was missing?

"Look!" cried Little Bear.

"Another clue!"

"Those look like Hen's tracks!"
said Owl.

Could Hen have taken the pie?

"If we follow the footprints,
we'll find Hen," said Little Bear.
"And I'll bet we'll find the pie!"
said Emily.

Little Bear followed the tracks

right up to his front door.

Little Bear opened the door,

and there sat Hen—

eating Father Bear's pie.

"Hello!" said Hen.

She had a beak full of pie.

"Hen, you are eating the pie!"

said Little Bear.

"And it is very good!" said Hen.

"But what will Father Bear say?"
Emily asked.

"I will say that there is enough pie

for everyone," said a deep voice.

Father Bear was home!

Little Bear ran to him.

Little Bear sat on Father Bear's lap.

"This pie tastes so much better

when I can share it with all of you,"

said Father Bear.

Everyone agreed.